Beatrice
AND
Vanessa

story by
John Yeoman

pictures by
Quentin Blake

MACMILLAN CHILDREN'S BOOKS

First published in Great Britain 1974 by Hamish
Hamilton Children's Books Ltd

Picturemac edition published 1988 by
Macmillan Children's Books
A division of Macmillan Publishers Limited
London and Basingstoke
Associated companies throughout the world

British Library Cataloguing in Publication Data
Yeoman, John
Beatrice and Vanessa
I. Title   II. Blake, Quentin
823′.914[J]   PZ7

ISBN 0-333-46779-5

Printed in Hong Kong

This is Beatrice

This is Vanessa

Beatrice, the ewe, and Vanessa, the nanny-goat, had spent their lives together in the same field. Every day for as long as they could remember they had nibbled the same grass, ambled slowly round the same farm buildings, rubbed their sides against the same tree, and stood nattering together with their chins resting on the same gate.

Today seemed specially dull. The grass was limp
and tasteless, and neither of them could think
of anything new to talk about.

"We shall have to take a holiday," said Vanessa
suddenly.
"Now?" asked Beatrice, who was much more
timid than her friend.
"There's no time like the present," said Vanessa,
"and we aren't getting any younger. Let's pack
straight away."

"But you know we haven't anything to pack,"
said Beatrice.

It was true. But Vanessa had another idea.
"We shall borrow one or two things from the
farmhouse," she said. "They had a party there
last night, so nobody will be up yet." Beatrice
looked uncertain. "After all," said Vanessa,
"we can always return the things when we come
back."
As they walked off to the silent farmhouse
to see what they could find, Beatrice was filled
with admiration for her clever friend.

As Vanessa had thought, there was no one about
in the farmhouse when they poked their heads
round the door into the hall.
"Do you see anything you fancy?" asked Vanessa.
Beatrice noticed a beautiful bunch of balloons
which had been tied on to a stuffed wolf's
head on the wall.
"They would make me feel on holiday," she
said in an excited voice.
"There doesn't seem much else besides this
old shopping bag on the table," said Vanessa.
"I suppose we might as well borrow that and
the wolf's head too."

Very quickly for her age, Vanessa clambered on
to the table and passed down the wolf's head
for Beatrice to pop into the shopping bag. Then
she freed the string of the balloons from
around its neck so that Beatrice could take
hold of it.

The two old friends crossed the farmyard and squeezed through a hole in the hedge they had known about for years, being very careful not to get the balloons tangled up. Then they set off from the farm for the first time in their lives.

They travelled slowly because they ate grass
all the time as they went along. It certainly
tasted sweeter and fresher than the farmyard
grass. Without noticing it, they nibbled
their way into a dark forest.

And then suddenly, to their alarm,
they looked up to find themselves
face to face with a pack of lean,
hungry wolves.
"Welcome, ladies," said the leader
of the wolves. "You are just in time
for dinner. Isn't that so, boys?"
And the whole pack of wolves
started chuckling.
Beatrice was so frightened of them
that she let go of her balloons, which
went floating up and away into
the forest. But she trusted her
sensible friend to think of something.

"Thank you for your kind invitation,
gentlemen," said Vanessa, "but I'm afraid
we're on a diet at the moment. But we'd
be delighted if you'd share our meal with us."
Then she turned to Beatrice and whispered
something in her ear.
"My friend will just have a look to see
if there is anything tasty in our bag," she said.
As Beatrice, with shaking hooves, began
to rummage in the bag, Vanessa added:
"Not the fat one, of course. And certainly
not the stale one."

Finally, Beatrice timidly lifted out the stuffed wolf's head.

"Wonderful," said Vanessa. "That's what I call a really fresh, juicy one. Have we six or seven more like that in there?"

Beatrice had no time to reply. There was
an ear-splitting howl as the terrified
wolves fled into the depths of the forest.

They ran and ran until at last they found
their path blocked by an enormous bear.

"What's the matter?" he asked.
"Is there a fire in the forest?"

All the wolves began explaining at once, but
finally the leader was able to tell the bear
what had frightened them.
"A ewe and a nanny-goat, eh?" said the bear,
licking his lips at the thought. "Well, if they
only eat wolves I've got nothing to worry about.
Just lead me to them and I'll take care
of them for you."
"They can't have gone far," said the wolf leader.
"They're terribly old."

At once the whole howling pack,
followed by the bear, turned round
and raced back through the forest.
The fearful noise they made sent all
the little forest animals scampering
ahead of them in alarm.
Beatrice and Vanessa were puzzled
to see a number of squirrels
streak past them.
"Up a tree, quickly," squealed the
squirrels. "The wolves are coming."

Although they didn't feel very happy about
climbing trees at their age, Beatrice and
Vanessa saw that it was the only thing to do.
"After all," said Vanessa, as she hoisted her
nervous friend on to a low branch, "they'll never
think of looking for us up a tree."

The fat bear, who was quite out of breath after his
long run, collapsed panting at the foot of the very tree
in which Beatrice and Vanessa were hiding.
He wiped his forehead with his paw. "You chaps
spread out and look for the ewe and the nanny-goat
while I sit here and organise things," he said.

At this moment
poor Beatrice, who was
having great difficulty
in keeping her balance
on her thin branch
above the bear's head,
felt herself slipping.

"I'm afraid I can't hold on
much longer," she whispered.

Vanessa knew that she must do something
immediately. Suddenly she noticed a piece of
string dangling through the leaves.
When she looked up she saw that Beatrice's
balloons had drifted into the next tree and
were stuck in a branch just above their heads.
"Don't panic, Beatrice," she said, reaching across
and pulling the balloons down very gently.
"Just do what I do."

When the balloons were within reach,
clever Vanessa began stabbing at them
with her little hooves, making them
explode:
        BANG!
                BANG!
                        BANG!
And they began shouting at the
tops of their voices:
        "There's a bear!"
                "Set the dogs loose!"
                        "Don't let him get away!"

Without knowing what was happening,
the bear and the pack of wolves fled off
again, howling, into the forest.

Vanessa clambered to the ground and
helped Beatrice down. Then with the
shopping bag and the wolf's head, but
without their balloons, they made their
way together out of the forest.

Back at the farm they still nibble the
same dry grass, rub their sides against
the same tree, and carry on their
never-ending conversation at the same gate.

But now they really have got something
to talk about.